The Desert Challenge

THE DESERT
CHALLENGE

BEAR GRYLLS
ILLUSTRATED BY EMMA McCANN

First American Edition 2017
Kane Miller, A Division of EDC Publishing

First published in Great Britain in 2017 by Bear Grylls, an imprint
of Bonnier Zaffre, a Bonnier Publishing Company
Text and illustrations copyright © Bear Grylls Ventures, 2017
Illustrations by Emma McCann

For information contact:
Kane Miller, A Division of EDC Publishing
PO Box 470663
Tulsa, OK 74147-0663
www.kanemiller.com
www.edcpub.com
www.usbornebooksandmore.com

Library of Congress Control Number: 2017945580

Printed and bound in the United States of America
2 3 4 5 6 7 8 9 10

ISBN: 978-1-61067-764-6

*To the young adventurer
reading this book for the first time.
May your eyes always be wide-open
to adventure, and your heart full
of courage and determination to
see your dreams through.*

1

NASTY INSECTS

Sophie was on a roll. As she pelted down the field with the rest of her five-a-side team, she thought that this had to be the best camp ever.

Sophie was on the Red team. The Yellows had a good defense going. Every time the Reds got the ball halfway to the other end of the field, the Yellows always managed to get hold of it and kick it back. Then the Reds would take it and run back toward the Yellows again.

That was how it had been for most of the game. They were in the last few minutes and the score was 0–0. Sophie suddenly saw her chance. She was about twelve feet from the goal.

Chloe had the ball over on the other side of the field, and Olivia, the defender on the Yellow team, was charging at her. Chloe gave the ball a desperate kick and hoped for the best.

The ball curved up into the air, toward Sophie.

Sophie timed her leap perfectly. She could have headed it, but headers weren't allowed in five-a-side. So she jumped up just as the ball was starting to come down. It bumped her in the chest and fell at her feet.

Sophie kicked the ball clean into the net.

"Goal!"

The ref blew her whistle, and the Reds had won, 1–0. The fans cheered.

The Yellows congratulated them. "Next time!" Olivia promised, with a big smile.

Sophie and Chloe wandered over to the touchline together, to get their things. Fatima, who shared their tent, had been watching and came over.

"Drink?" Chloe offered Sophie a bottle of juice.

Just as Sophie took it she saw movement in the corner of her eye.

The wasp came straight at her out of nowhere.

Sophie couldn't help it. She screamed,

and jerked her entire body away from the insect. Juice squirted all over Fatima.

The wasp flew off.

"Aack!" Fatima stared down at her soaked front.

"I'm so sorry!" Sophie blurted.

"It's not your fault." Fatima tried to put a good face on it. "Anyone can be afraid of wasps." She looked down at herself again. "But it was my last clean shirt …"

"You can have one of mine from the tent," Sophie promised.

"You don't have to," Fatima said.

"Yes," Sophie insisted. "Yes, I do."

She started back to their tent and was soon away from all the other kids. She could still hear them through the trees. Everyone was laughing and chatting and shouting – all the usual things.

But she was all on her own by the time she reached her tent. She didn't like being alone in there.

Sophie almost chickened out, until she remembered she had made Fatima a promise. She *would* get that shirt.

Her heart pounded and her mouth was dry. She leaned forward, took a breath, and pulled the zipper open.

Inside, all the girls' gear was in jumbled piles. It was how they had left it that morning. Sophie's stuff was farthest from the flap so she had to climb over her friends' things. She rummaged inside the bag.

"I know you'll get them all wet and dirty," Mom had said. "So make sure you take a few."

Sophie scrambled through the pile

until she had a shirt for Fatima.

She turned to go, at the exact moment that her worst fears came true.

A crane fly came bumbling in through the flap.

2

DADDY LONGLEGS

Sophie shrieked, and threw herself back to get away from the insect. The whole tent shook.

She tried to hide in a corner, making herself as small as possible. The crane fly swung from side to side in the air, like it was trying to block her escape.

"Go away," she begged it. But the insect stayed put, fussing around like it couldn't decide whether to go up or down or whatever.

Then suddenly it was gone. She had only taken her eyes off it for a moment and now it had vanished. But she was almost certain that it hadn't gone out. That meant it was *still in the tent*. It was somewhere between her and the flap. It was perched on someone's sleeping bag, or on top of a discarded hoodie or a pair of shoes.

"Okay," Sophie said with clenched teeth, "it's just a daddy longlegs. I am not going to be beaten by a spider with wings."

All she wanted was for it to stay in one place, so she could get out and get on with her day.

Sophie held her breath and started to crawl for the flap. She moved an arm.

Nothing happened. She moved a leg, then another arm. She shifted forward a bit. Still no daddy longlegs.

Maybe it had gone to sleep?

She moved her other arm, and the crane fly took off right in front of her.

Sophie flung herself back without thinking and with a scream. The tent shook again.

This was ridiculous. She had to be about a million times bigger than the nasty insect. Why was she so afraid?

There was nothing for it. She didn't want to hurt it, but she didn't have a choice if she was going to get out of the tent that afternoon.

Sophie picked up a heap of clothes and flung them over where she had last

11

spotted the crane fly. Then she crawled forward as quickly as she could, plowing her way through the other girls' things to get to the entrance.

But the flap had closed. The Velcro tabs had gotten stuck together. Sophie almost sobbed as she scrabbled to get it open. She was sure it was behind her, ready to crawl down her neck …

She tugged at the flap so hard it almost tore, but then it was open. Sophie shot out of the tent like soda out of a bottle. She only just remembered to grab the clean shirt for Fatima on the way. It would have been too bad to forget it and have to start all over again.

Once she was safely outside she wanted to kick something. She was so angry with herself. Why did she always do this with bugs? Why? Why? Why?

Sophie drew several deep breaths to calm herself down. But, deep down inside, she wanted to burst into tears. She *hated* this! She hated feeling so helpless. She *knew* a daddy longlegs was harmless.

But horrible spiders and insects just made her feel sick, and there was nothing she could do about it. She hated them all. Spiders, wasps, bees, beetles, caterpillars, earwigs …

"I mean, what is the point?" she shouted. She wasn't shouting at anyone in particular. Just bugs in general. "Bees … okay, bees make honey. But, you know, you could probably grow honey in a lab or something. What about all the others?

What is the point of nasty insects that buzz around in the way?"

That was when she realized a boy was there, looking at her. She turned bright red.

Normally, when someone saw her being frightened of an insect, she tried to make a joke of it. She would say something like, "Wow, that gave me a shock, I thought it was something else," and give a little laugh.

It was too late for that now. He would have heard everything. He must have wondered what all the fuss was about.

"What do you want?" she snapped.

He looked at her like she was weird in some way and he was too polite to point it out. Now she remembered seeing him before. They'd been gathering logs to build dens at the woodpile, and she had screamed when she saw a spider. He had heard her then as well … Sophie felt her toes curling with embarrassment.

"I just want to give you this," he said gently. "It's a gift." He held out his hand with something in it.

"What is it?" Sophie asked.

"Your adventure," he replied.

Sophie was still annoyed, but she was curious, so she took what he was offering. It was a small plastic pocket compass. Nothing special.

"Uh – thanks, I guess."

"I mean," he added, "it helped me. It really did." He gave her a hopeful smile, and then hurried off.

Sophie stared after him. Then she shrugged, and stuck the compass in her pocket.

She had the new shirt for Fatima, which was the main thing. But she was still furious with herself and those horrible insects.

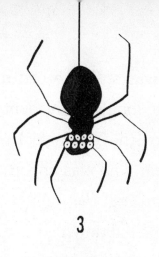

3

SANDPIT

"Come on, slowpoke! The Reds are getting ahead!"

Sophie and Fatima were in the obstacle relay race. One person from each team had to race with a baton between two obstacles, and then hand it over to the next runner. This time Sophie was on the Yellow team. The Reds had handed over their baton slightly faster than the Yellows, and now Sophie had to catch up.

Sophie was still in a bad mood after the daddy longlegs incident. It didn't help that on the Yellow team was a boy called Omar who was impatient with … well, everything.

Sophie pelted down her stretch of the track through the woods. Sometimes she pulled a little bit ahead of the Red boy. Sometimes he got a little ahead of her.

The track twisted and turned between the trees, so everyone's teammates could dash to the next handover point and get there before the runners, to cheer them on. But Omar didn't cheer. Nothing was good enough for him.

They were coming to the next obstacle. Each one was different. So, once the runners had to crawl under a fallen tree, and another time, they had to climb up a rope ladder, tied around a branch, and down the other side. (Sophie was glad she hadn't gotten the first one – all sorts of small things lived under logs.)

Some obstacles meant you had to use your mind rather than your body, like saying the alphabet backward. They always had to complete the obstacle

before handing over the baton. There was a surprise challenge for the very last obstacle – the one that the last runner would have to overcome if they wanted to win. So she was quite glad Chloe had offered to go last.

Sophie's obstacle was a deep sandpit. She ran up to it, with the boy from the other team hot on her heels. Fatima was waiting for the baton on the other side. The pit was about two hundred feet across and there were two zip lines, one for each team. Each zip line had a metal pole hanging from the cable, with a seat at its end.

Sophie pelted up to her pole while Omar ran alongside her, shouting at her to move faster. Sophie stuck the baton inside her pocket, grabbed the pole in both hands, and kicked off from the edge of the pit.

The zip line buzzed as she hurtled along it. The Red boy was just behind her. Sophie grinned as the air rushed past her head. She could win this!

About a quarter of the way across the pit, she felt something shift in her pocket. The baton was about to fall! She quickly took one hand off the pole so that she could push it back into her pocket. She didn't want to lose it and have to start again. But instead of the baton, her fingertips touched something flat. *Of course*, she remembered, *it*

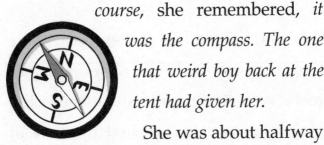

was the compass. The one that weird boy back at the tent had given her.

She was about halfway

across the pit, right over the deepest part.

Something glinted in the air in front of her. She had half a second to see it.

It was a single strand of spider's web, shining in the sun. Coming straight at her face.

Sophie shrieked the loudest shriek *ever*, and tried to twist on the pole to dodge it. She only had one hand on the pole, but she panicked and let go, waving it frantically in front of her face to push the web away. The compass and baton went flying through the air. She tried to grab at the pole again, but her body was twisting and turning and her fingers bounced off the metal.

She was going to fall.

Everything seemed to be happening in slow motion. The compass spun in the air in front of her eyes. She could see North, South, East and West and … a fifth direction? The dial seemed to grow bigger as it flew closer to her face. In fact, she seemed to be falling *through* the dial.

Sophie plowed facefirst into the sand and ended up with a mouthful of the stuff.

"*Bleurgh*!"

The sand was dry and gritty and disgusting. She spat it out. *Honestly*, she thought furiously, *what kind of person can't even sit on a zip line?* She'd never felt so hot and embarrassed.

It was all that horrible spider's fault …

But she really was *hot*. Her eyes were still screwed tightly shut to keep the sand out, but the sun seemed extra bright. So bright that there was a red glow through her eyelids.

Sophie brushed the sand carefully away from her face before opening her eyes. For some reason she couldn't hear any of the other campers. Perhaps she had sand in her ears too. She knew everyone would be laughing at her. Except Omar, who would just be angry.

She opened her eyes. And suddenly a very bright light flooded in.

"Ow!" she exclaimed.

She squeezed her eyes tightly shut again, then opened them a crack, slowly.

And then her eyes grew wide.

She realized why she couldn't hear the others. It was because they weren't there. She wasn't in the sandpit at camp. But she *was* standing in sand. It was smooth and yellow.

Miles and miles

of it. A desert. All the way to the horizon. The air shimmered in the baking heat.

She jumped when a man's voice spoke, right behind her.

"Hey! Get over here, before the sun bakes your brains out!"

4

GIANT SPIDERS

Sophie turned around in surprise. A couple of rocks and a very tired-looking palm tree stuck out of the sand behind her. The tree cast a shadow about the size of a tablecloth, and that was where the man was sitting, with his backpack next to him.

His tanned face was pleasant and friendly.

"Desert temperatures can get up to

more than one hundred twenty degrees," he added. "Come into the shade."

Despite the talk about baking her brains out, his voice sounded calming.

Sophie still had no idea how she had gotten here, but the desert heat was inside her as well as out. Every breath of scorching air made her lungs glow. She peeled her hoodie off and went toward the shade.

The man sat quietly, looking out at the shimmering desert. The sky was bright blue without a cloud in it. The horizon was a long way away.

Eventually, Sophie asked, "Where am I?"

"Well, it looks like you're on a journey…" He paused, then looked straight at her. "And I'm here to help you."

Then he looked away into the far distance.

Sophie was puzzled.

"A journey to where?" she asked.

The man pointed at the horizon.

"Out of the desert," he said with a smile. "Ready for some *real* adventure?"

Sophie looked around at the baking sands. No sign of any kind of transportation.

"You mean, walk?"

"That's right."

This was the weirdest thing that had ever happened to Sophie. But the man didn't seem surprised to see her, and he said he wanted to help her get back. She knew she couldn't do it on her own, so she decided to trust him.

She looked down at the clothes she

had been wearing for the race. Hoodie, T-shirt and shorts.

"Well, I guess I'm dressed for the beach," she said lightly.

He frowned. "Mmm ... No. Your skin's too exposed. You want something light and loose enough for the air to circulate next to your skin to cool you down, but strong enough to stop the desert wind peeling your skin off your body. Here."

He rummaged in his backpack and

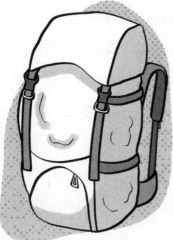 pulled out a long-sleeved shirt, a pair of tough cotton pants, and some boots like his, all in her size. Then he turned his back so she could get changed.

"Looks like you were somehow prepared for me to be here?" Sophie asked.

"Your journey has been calling for a while, I suspect," he replied.

Sophie didn't reply. She didn't really know what he meant.

When she was changed, Sophie asked, "So, when do we start walking?"

She wasn't really looking forward to this – it was so hot and dry she couldn't imagine how they'd ever manage it.

"What does the sky tell you?" he asked.

She looked up again.

The sun wasn't high up. The horizon was starting to turn red, like sunset.

"It must be close to evening," she guessed, "so ... we wait until the morning?"

He smiled.

"We start now. It's too hot to walk while the sun's so strong in the midday heat, so we travel at the start and the end of the day. I've been waiting here since this morning. Here, take a drink before we get going."

He passed over a battered leather canteen.

"Take small mouthfuls," he told her. "Hold them in your mouth to let them soak in. *Then* swallow."

"Thank you, um ..." She had just realized she didn't know his name. "I'm

Sophie," she said, as she took the canteen.

"Pleased to meet you. I'm Bear."

They shook hands, and Sophie took a drink. The water was slightly warm and musty tasting, but still refreshing.

Just then, Sophie saw an absolutely *massive* spider crawling across the sand toward her. It was about four inches across. Its legs were long and hairy, and its jaws were so big that she could see them.

She shrieked and leaped away. Water sprayed out of the canteen.

"Hey!" Bear quickly grabbed the canteen from her and screwed it shut. "Careful, Sophie. Water is our most precious resource out here. We can go a few weeks if we have to without food, but without water we'll die within a few days at most."

"I'm sorry ..." Sophie gasped. She was furious with herself again. It was so embarrassing. But she was also terrified.

"What's that?" she said, pointing at the spider. It was still crawling toward her. She took a couple of steps to get farther away.

Bear leaned close to it.

"Camel spider," he said. "Not a real spider. Not a real camel either, for that matter. More like a scorpion. It's just after the shade, like everything else out here. Always remember – if you find a nice shady nook to sit in, chances are good that something else already has."

"Is it poisonous?" she asked.

"Just painful. Its bite wouldn't kill you. Not like lack of water would."

He looked at her with a wry smile, and she blushed. Meanwhile the camel spider had reached the bottom of the tree. It dug itself a small hole in the sand and vanished.

Sophie made sure she knew exactly where

it was, so she could avoid it.

"Hey," Bear said, "here's a couple of useful tricks for the survivor who's traveling light. When you don't have sunglasses or sunscreen, this is the next best thing."

He dug his fingers deep into the sand and dirt and worked them around  until they were grimy. Then he smeared the paste in two splodges on his face, under his eyes. Sophie thought it made him look like a panda.

"This reduces the sun glare that gets into your eyes. And then ..."

He rubbed each hand over the back of the other one to smudge the dirt onto them as well.

"This protects your exposed skin. And while you do that, I've got something else for your head and face."

Sophie dug for some dirt of her own, and Bear got a cotton scarf with a colorful pattern of squares, and rows of knots along each side, out of his backpack.

"This is a shemagh," he said. "Here's how you put it on …"

Bear showed her how to wrap the shemagh around her head so that there was just a slit for her eyes.

She could lift up the front if she needed to drink or eat. Then he did the same for himself.

She looked out at the desert again through the slit. "At least out there in the sun there won't be any giant spiders," she muttered to herself.

Bear laughed.

"That's maybe true. But plenty of other wildlife out there can kill us." He paused. "Ready?"

5

WATER TRICK

"Do you have a compass?" Bear asked. His voice was muffled by his shemagh.

"Oh. Yes." Sophie had forgotten about it. She held it up, and remembered how it had seemed to grow bigger and change. But now the dial just had the usual four directions.

She stared at it confused. Then looked up at Bear, then across to the desert.

"Did this ... did this compass somehow

bring me here?" she asked quietly.

Bear looked at her. "Maybe. But what I do know is that it can get us out. Just point us north by northwest."

Sophie turned the compass.

She pointed. "That way."

"Nice. We'll walk a little so you can begin to get used to the desert heat and terrain. We walk slow and easy, to avoid sweating more than we have to, but we also take firm, steady steps to scare off any snakes."

"Snakes?"

Sophie whipped her head around, staring madly at the sand in every direction. If there was one thing she hated more than spiders and insects, it was *snakes.*

She thought Bear was probably smiling

behind his shemagh as he settled his backpack on his back.

"Walk properly and you'll never see them. Meanwhile, breathe through your nose, and no shouting, to stop your mouth drying out. Ready? Then, onward!"

They set off in the direction the compass had shown.

Walking north by northwest meant that the setting sun was on their left, and the sky was lit with amazing curtains of red and orange light.

The walking was hard, though. Not like Sophie had been used to back home, where you just walk and don't need to think about it. Here was different. Very different.

The sand was always slipping and sliding beneath Sophie. There was nothing to get a grip on – it was kind of like when she had played soccer on the beach.

An ache started to grow deep inside her legs. But she was terrified by the idea of snakes, and so she made sure she plonked a foot down firmly with every step.

Bear followed the low ground between the dunes, where the sand was flat, so they were in the shade. He called a halt after about ten minutes.

"Got the hang of it? Good. Now, here's a smart trick. I learned this from the Tarahumara tribe in Mexico." He handed her the canteen. "Take a mouthful of water ... and keep it there. No swallowing. Breathe through your nose. The water soaks into your body and the mouthful lasts a lot longer. You'll find you really want to swallow, so at first we'll just try it for a minute to start with, okay? And we'll do it every half hour. With a bit of practice you'll be holding it in for ages, like the Tarahumara do."

He set the alarm on his watch.

"Okay ... go."

Sophie raised the canteen and a mouthful of warm water flooded her dry mouth.

"Just breathe," Bear said, "and walk."

Sophie almost spat the water out in the first few seconds. She had to concentrate on holding it in *and* walking the way Bear had told her. Whenever it sloshed against the back of her mouth it made her want to swallow, but she resisted.

At least it took her mind off her aching legs.

Because the route was winding through the dunes they couldn't stick to the same direction all the time. Bear asked her regularly to check her compass to make sure they were heading roughly the right way.

Then they came around the side of a dune and saw that the way ahead was blocked. The only way forward was to go up a steep slope of sand. A massive sheer sand dune.

"Okay, we're going to need all our concentration to

get up that thing," Bear said.

"Dunes look solid, but they're really just big piles of sand that the wind blows into shapes. There's nothing to hold them together, and all they really want to do is fall down. As you'll find out. Coming?"

Not sure what he meant, Sophie started to walk side by side with Bear. And walk. And walk. Loose sand tumbled down over her boots with every step.

After a few moments, she couldn't help noticing something.

She wasn't going anywhere.

Bear was getting farther in front of her.

She started to take extra-long steps, and now she *was* moving. Backward. Bear was getting even farther away.

The ground slid from beneath her and

she fell flat on her face.

"It moves!" she exclaimed.

"We'll try a shallower angle," Bear suggested, "so that the sides are less inclined to collapse under our weight."

They changed direction so that now they were walking more along the dune, and only a little bit up. When they had reached the edge, they turned around and went the other way. And so they slowly zigzagged their way to the top.

Sophie reckoned that if this had been a hill back home, she could have run up it in a few seconds. Here it must have taken something like twenty minutes. Half a math class at least.

At long last they reached the top. Sophie's legs were throbbing with the extra effort.

"Whew!" Sophie gasped. "Will there be more like that?"

"That's up to the desert." Bear checked the compass over Sophie's shoulder. "It's a shallower slope on this side since it faces into the wind. That'll make it easier to get down."

They started walking again, toward the last glow of the sunset. Soon that vanished. The sky was black and the stars began to appear. A half-moon showed above the horizon and the desert became silver with its light.

Although Sophie had been baking hot during the day, now she wasn't. She rubbed her arms. Her skin under her shirt had goose bumps.

"B-Bear," she began, and stopped in surprise. Her teeth were chattering.

"Cold?" he asked. She nodded. He stooped down so that she could get into his backpack and pull out the hoodie she had been wearing when she arrived here. She put it on, but the desert air was still cold enough to bite.

Her shemagh no longer kept the sun's heat out, it was keeping her head's warmth in. But still she shivered.

"How can I be freezing cold in the middle of the desert?"

"Night air keeps its warmth because there's moisture in the air to store it, or clouds to stop it radiating away into space," Bear said. "But here there are no clouds or moisture. All that lovely heat that the air got from the sun during the day gets lost, and there's no sun to replace it."

"You can't freeze to death in the middle of the desert, though ..." Sophie said. "Can you?"

"A hundred percent, we can," Bear said seriously. "Bake your brains out during the day, freeze them solid at night. But I think I see what we need ..."

ROCK RADIATORS

Up ahead, Sophie saw black shadows splashed across the sand like poster paint. They were walking into a field of rocks and stones from the size of soccer balls to refrigerators.

Bear flicked a flashlight on and the beam splashed across the rocks.

"We have to think calmly and laterally out here," he announced quietly. "You're cold? We get the rocks to warm you up."

Sophie touched one of them. The rough surface was warm.

"But the sun went down hours ago!"

"And these rocks stored its heat," Bear told her. "Like a storage heater. And we won't let it go to waste. Here, hold this. Shine it at the base."

He passed her the flashlight, wrapped his arms around the large rock and tilted it up.

"Anything underneath?"

Sophie remembered his remark about always checking shady nooks. She supposed that if crawly, snappy, bitey creatures went under them during the day to get out of the sun, they might do the same at night for the warmth.

So there might be something crawly or snappy or bitey down there now …

Her breath was coming quickly, in short pants. She didn't want to look.

"You can do it, Sophie," Bear said, still holding up the rock.

Sophie swallowed, hard, and shone the flashlight underneath.

There wasn't anything there.

"Nothing," she said.

"Okay. Good!" Bear grunted. He let the rock drop back, and just as he did, the flashlight caught something scuttle out from a small rock next to it.

It was a scorpion, and it was waving its claws right at Sophie.

She jumped back with a loud scream.

It was like a cross between a giant spider and a lobster, about the length of her longest finger. It had two big claws, and a stinger on a tail that curved over its head to point forward. She dropped the flashlight in her panic.

Everything was suddenly dark. The scorpion could be creeping up on her, waving its claws, getting closer ...

"It's okay, Sophie. Just keep calm and step back." Bear picked the flashlight up and shone it on the scorpion, still on the rock. "Better it's out here and we know about it. Some scorpions are highly venomous and can easily kill you, but this is dangerous but not deadly. Still, it's not something we want nearby while we rest." He paused. "Remember: everything here is locked in a battle to survive – like us."

He pulled out his knife and killed it calmly and quickly, then cut off the stinger on its tail and put the scorpion in his pocket.

"What we kill, we eat," Bear said.

"You have to be joking," Sophie announced.

"Not at all. The desert can kill you, but it can also provide. Now let's get to it, Sophie – step one is to build a camp. Shine the flashlight over here …"

Sophie shook her head in half disgust and half shock, but together they started to make the camp.

With Sophie lighting the ground, Bear built a low, U-shaped rock wall. They studied each rock from every angle in case of any more scorpions. Then Bear laid down a groundsheet inside the wall so they could sit on the sand. To Sophie's surprise, he also started to build a fire.

"Where did that come from?" she asked.

"The palm tree at the oasis. It's just dry wood that fell off. In survival we always look around for stuff to use. Most people walk past the simplest of things that could save their life."

Sophie thought back to where she had met Bear.

"That was an oasis?" she said. Her local swimming pool was called the Oasis. It had lots of little pools and chutes and fountains, and water everywhere.

"Sure," he said with a chuckle. "How do you think the tree managed to grow? There was water below the sand. That's where I filled the canteen from. I'll show you tomorrow."

Bear pulled a couple of pieces of metal from a chain on his neck and struck them together. They sprayed sparks onto the wood, and soon the smallest of flames caught the dry husks of the palm tree.

Within seconds a small fire was crackling away.

Bear pulled out the remains of the scorpion from his pocket and put them on the end of his knife.

Then he held it over the flames and it
started to sizzle.

"First scorpion, I imagine?" he asked
Sophie.

"Um. Yes. It's not exactly on my

normal supper menu." Sophie looked a bit worried.

"It's like most things we fear," Bear said.

"What do you mean?"

"I mean that the taste isn't too bad, actually. It is just our fear that tells us it will be awful. Same with most other things," Bear told her. "When we face up to the thing we are scared of, we often find it isn't so bad." He paused. "Here, try it!"

"Really? I don't think I can."

"Well, just try. Let's have half each. It's only tiny, but it will warm us up, give us a small hit of protein and go some way to helping you over your fears, maybe."

That makes sense, Sophie thought.

"I guess," she said.

"We'll eat it at the same time," Bear said as he handed Sophie half of the remains of the scorpion's body. "One, two, three ..."

To her surprise the scorpion didn't actually taste much different than the burned sausages at camp. She smiled at Bear and kept chewing.

"Well, it's not great ... but it isn't too bad, I figure."

"Good for you, girl!"

They drank water and ate a couple of energy bars as well as the scorpion, and the air around them grew warm as the fire's heat reflected off the inside of the U-shaped wall.

Although she was exhausted from walking, after the freezing cold of the desert at night, Sophie felt like she had just had a hot bath …

Sophie didn't remember going to sleep, but she woke hours later, curled up on the groundsheet. The sky was gray, but the horizon was lit up with yellow and red light. Sunrise in the desert.

The fire had gone out, as the last of the wood that Bear had carried in his backpack had run out. It was cold. But not as cold as it had been in the middle of the night. The dawn was coming and with it the heat would soon be upon them.

Bear sat on the ground, staring calmly out into the desert.

"Morning," he said cheerfully. "A quick bite of breakfast and then we push on. We can do another three, four hours before it gets too hot."

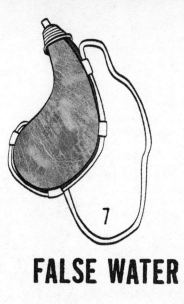

7

FALSE WATER

Sand, sand, and, oh look, more sand, Sophie thought as they walked.

They were doing the hold-the-water-in-your-mouth thing again. The water mixed with her spit and turned warm and sticky.

But she kept it in.

"Five minutes," Bear said eventually. "You can swallow now."

They had started out holding the water

in their mouths for a minute and they were now progressing. She was getting better at it. Sophie gratefully gulped it down.

After that they walked in silence. Talking just used up moisture.

When Sophie had arrived in the desert the day before, it was the late afternoon. Even though it had been amazingly hot the day had been getting *cooler*.

Now the desert was warming up, like someone was turning up the dial on an oven.

Yesterday they had walked in the shadows of the dunes. Today they still kept to the low ground, but as the sun got higher it shone directly on them. The air ahead began to shimmer in the heat. Sophie could feel the sun battering against her clothes and the shemagh over her head.

But even though she wasn't exactly cool, she didn't overheat. Air flowed between her clothes and her skin, like Bear had said it would.

Just then, a streak of white light flashed in front of her eyes. There was a clear silver band stretching across the horizon.

"A lake!" she exclaimed. She'd never felt so happy to see water in her life – they must be nearly out of the desert.

Bear was already shaking his head.

"Keep looking," he said.

Sophie blinked in surprise as the silver band shriveled into silver spots, and then vanished.

But in its place there *was* something

real. It looked like a pile of fur rugs lying in the sand. It looked sort of familiar, but Sophie couldn't say what it was. She ran its shape through her head, trying to match it with something.

It wasn't until they were right up close that she finally realized.

"Oh, *gross!*"

It was a camel.
A dead one. Long dead.
Its dried-up flesh had
shrink-wrapped itself
around its bones. Its
hair had fallen off in thick,
dirty clumps and
there were
gaping holes in what
was left of its body.
And one of those
holes seemed to
be moving …
She shrieked and leaped back.
"Oh, that is so disgusting!"
The hole was absolutely crawling
with maggots.
"Disgusting
maybe, but good

news for us," Bear commented casually. "There's good energy in maggots."

She stared at him.

"You'd eat maggots?"

"In the desert and trying to stay alive, yes. There's great protein in a maggot, and you can use them for many other things too. You can use them as bait, and they can keep a wound clean …

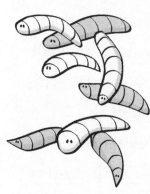

Don't knock a maggot."

Sophie made herself look again at the maggots, crawling in the dead camel. She tried to see them through Bear's eyes.

Useful?

"Our priority out here isn't food, though. There's a rule of three: three minutes without air, three days without water, three weeks without food. In this desert it's a lack of water that will kill us first," Bear explained. "Otherwise we'd be having a maggot feast!" He chuckled. "But not today. The priority for us is to keep moving."

"Phew!" Sophie was very relieved.

They walked for another forty-five minutes while the desert grew even hotter. Sophie started to feel like the heat was a solid obstacle and she was pushing her way through it.

The ground was growing hard and rocky.

A couple of minutes later they were standing on the edge of a small ravine, about fifteen feet deep and seventy across. The rocky sides were steep, but they could climb down them. The bottom was flat sand, with smooth rocks scattered along it.

Large parts of the bottom of the ravine were in shadow.

"We'll shelter in this wadi until the heat of midday has come and gone," Bear decided. "We've done enough for now. We survive by taking our time and playing it smart. Out here if you rush and don't think your actions through, you die."

"Yes. And we don't want to die," Sophie added with a dry look at Bear. "Anyway, what's a wadi?" she asked as they climbed down the side.

"It's a dry riverbed," he told her. "I've seen places like this go from not a drop of moisture to a raging river torrent within minutes. A flash flood. People drown in them, as they hit fast and with huge power. But above all because if people don't see water, they aren't prepared for water. So, if you hear me shout 'start climbing,' just trust me – and climb!"

Sophie could tell from Bear's voice that he wasn't kidding, but she was puzzled.

"But how could it flood? There's no water in a desert – you keep saying it's lack of water that will kill us."

"Imagine there is a lot of rain in the mountains, maybe fifty miles away at the source of the river," Bear explained. "Because the ground is baked so hard, the water doesn't drain away into the earth. So it comes rushing along the wadi instead. See those smooth rocks? They've been worn smooth by water."

As Bear seemed to be happy to talk now that they were out of the sun, Sophie tried another question.

"So what was that I saw earlier?" she asked, remembering the silver flash that had seemed like a lake.

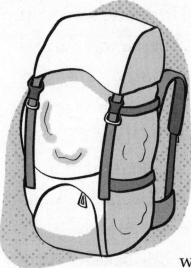

"Just a simple mirage. Hot air bends light. This air is so hot it reflects all the light straight back at you, like a mirror. You would see the same thing on a road, back home, if it was a superhot day."

He dumped his backpack down and passed her the groundsheet.

"I'm going to look for water. You see if you can find us a good spot to rest."

Sophie looked along the dry, empty canyon, but she couldn't see any sign of where there might be water. And she was a little surprised that Bear trusted her to find a place. But he seemed to be confident about both things, so she just went with it.

"Uh – sure," she said.

Sophie started looking, slowly at first. She remembered the rule about always checking for desert creatures that might be hidden in nooks and crannies, so she moved any rocks very carefully, and braced herself in case something was there. And she stamped her feet to spook off any snakes.

She found just the place at the foot of a small cliff at the side of the wadi. The compass said it faced

north, so it would always be in shadow as the sun moved around during the day. She studied it carefully for any unwanted visitors, and flicked the groundsheet out.

Just as she was about to lay the sheet down, she saw it. Right in front of her. Its yellow color had made it blend into the sand.

It was a creature out of Sophie's nightmares. An enormous snake, coiled, and staring right at her.

Sophie froze. She didn't want to move, in case it attacked her.

"Bear!" she called loudly. She was scared, but she suddenly realized she also felt strangely calm. It was like the desert was changing her for the better, making her tougher. She was learning to deal with shock and trauma like someone who could handle the pressure of the desert. She was a survivor now.

Bear came hurrying over.

"A puff adder," he said immediately. "Well done – you've found one of the most venomous snakes in the world. But remember, they are only dangerous

if they bite you. So keep still and never take your eyes off it." He gently grabbed her hand and led her backward. "So I guess we won't be resting there, Sophie!"

Sophie smiled.

"I guess it's like you said: everything here is locked in a battle to survive."

8

EMPTY RIVER

Sophie and Bear moved farther along the dry wadi looking for another, less "occupied" bit of shade in which to shelter. As they neared a shallow curve in the riverbed, Bear stopped and crouched at the outside edge of the bend.

"Let me show you how to find water," he said.

"Um, how exactly?" replied Sophie.

"Well, do you notice anything?" Bear asked.

Sophie looked around. All she could see were more rocks and an ugly, twisted little thorn bush.

She was about to say she couldn't see anything, when she remembered what he had said about the palm tree back at the oasis.

"That thorn bush must be getting water from somewhere," she said.

Bear gave her a smile.

"Correct. And, you see we're on the outside bend of the wadi? Where the flowing water has made the channel deepest? When the river was flowing it would have stayed wet here longer than anywhere else. In fact, the water should still be here …"

He started to dig with his bare hands.

The sand was dry and loose, and the sides of his little pit kept trickling back down to fill it in. Bear widened the pit and kept digging.

"The water, if it is here, will be maybe a foot or so under the surface," he said. "If it isn't, then it's not worth going deeper."

Sophie could see that the sand got darker as he went down, and suddenly she could *smell* damp. There was a kind of wet-stone whiff to the pit that made her think of sidewalks after the rain.

"There!" Sophie said.

There was a tiny speck of water at the bottom of the pit. It didn't look like much at all. Certainly not enough to fill a canteen with. But it was growing. It welled up, taking over the sand, grain by grain.

Bear stood up, looking pleased.

"We'll let it fill in its own time." He paused. "You see, Sophie – it's all about being smart. We've chosen our battles out here. We moved away from that puff adder, we found the shade, we dug this hole – and now it's time for nature to do its part."

Sophie nodded. "And we're surviving," she said.

"That's right," Bear replied. "Many other things out here don't. Including some humans. Think about it: most of us have two arms and two legs, a set of lungs and a beating heart. But not everyone will make it out here because we all make different decisions. Just always be patient and avoid danger where possible, but when it is time to work hard and fight, then give it your all. That's how to survive the desert."

They found a new spot for the groundsheet, tucked against the edge of the bank, nicely in the shade, and settled down to wait out the hottest part of the day.

"Sophie," Bear said quietly, "can I ask you something?"

"Sure," Sophie replied.

"I noticed that you screamed when you first saw the camel spider and the scorpion, and the maggots, but not when you saw the puff adder. What changed?"

"I guess it's because ..." Sophie thought. "Because I knew I had to deal with it to survive. I mean, compared to everything else, it was nothing. This is the *desert*. It's way bigger and nastier than any bug. You either get on with it or you get hurt. Plus, it becomes easier the more you do it."

He grinned.

"You're turning into a survivor, Sophie. Good for you. Respect." He paused. "Like I said, the best way over your fears is straight through the middle."

89

"And like you said, even things like maggots can be useful," Sophie added. "I guess everything's got its purpose even if we don't know what it is. So, why get upset about it, when it's just doing its thing?"

"That's life, eh?"

The sun moved slowly across the sky and the shadow of the cliff stretched itself out across the wadi. At long last, Bear stood up, stretched, and went over to inspect the water hole. It was almost full.

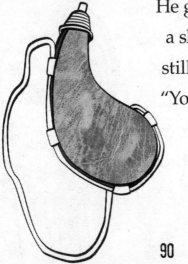

He gave the canteen a shake. There was still a little left in it. "You know the best place to carry water?" he said. "Inside you."

So they drank down what was left in the canteen together. Then Bear held it under the surface and let it refill, with many glugs and gurgles.

Then they wrapped their shemaghs around their heads and climbed together up the far side of the wadi to continue their trek.

Sophie clambered to her feet at the top, and blinked in surprise.

There was a mountain range ahead. It looked seriously high. She could see snow at the top of some of the peaks. It hadn't been there when Sophie and Bear had climbed down into the wadi.

"Now, *that* is a sight," Bear said.

"So are those mountains a mirage?"

"Oh no, they exist, but they're a hundred miles away," Bear said. "The hot air bends the light and seems to plonk them down in front of us. I'll show you."

He headed over to a large rock at the edge of the wadi, and leaped up it with a couple of quick steps. He stood three feet above the desert and held his hand out to help her up.

"Come and see."

Sophie took his hand and clambered up to stand beside him. The mountains wavered and wiggled, and then melted back into the distance.

"You just have to be a little bit higher or lower and the optical illusion stops working," he said, jumping down off the rock. "Nature is pretty cool, eh? And weird sometimes."

"I had no idea just how weird," Sophie replied. "Weird but wonderful."

She crouched down and stuck one leg out to reach the sand, but her other boot caught on a bump in the rock. With a shout of alarm she plowed facefirst into the sand.

"*Sophie? Sophie! Are you okay?*"

"I'm fine," she said, through a mouthful of sand. She spat it out and worked her mouth to get more saliva going. She had to blink fast to get the sand out of her eyes.

And then suddenly she was staring with astonishment at a worried-looking Fatima.

9

HANDOVER

"Sophie, are you okay?" Fatima said. "You were really moving fast when you fell off."

Sophie looked around. She was on her hands and knees in the sandpit at camp. Two zip lines ran overhead. Her pole was a few feet away, shaking and waving from side to side, as if she had just fallen off it. The Reds were just handing the baton over to the next person. Everyone was shouting and cheering.

"Come on, Sophie!"

The other Yellows were waiting at the end of the zip line, urging her on, shouting and waving their hands. She was dazed but didn't have time to work out how all this had happened. The race was still on and she was holding things up.

Sophie picked the baton up. And then she remembered that she was meant to be passing it on to Fatima. She started to hand it over, but Fatima was already running for the edge of the pit.

"You have to give it to me in the right place," she called over her shoulder. Sophie stumbled quickly after her to the end of the zip line, where the handover would have been if Sophie hadn't fallen.

Fatima grabbed the baton and ran off after the Reds. "You really held us up!" a boy shouted at her. It took Sophie a moment to remember his name. Oh, yes – Omar. "Can't you even stay on a zip line?

He hurried off with the others to the next handover point. *Probably to shout at someone else*, Sophie thought.

Now that she had a moment to herself, she looked back at the sandpit.

It was … sandy.

Apart from that, it didn't look at all like a desert. It was too small and too damp. The sand was a dark, wettish orange – not the amazing, blazing yellow she had gotten used to. The sun wasn't threatening to melt her brains out. It was politely asking the clouds if they would maybe mind giving it a bit of space. And she probably wouldn't find any lethal scorpions or rotting camels, however hard she looked.

Where had it all gone?

Something glistened in the sand, next to the small crater she had made when she fell off. Oh yes, the compass. She picked it up. She seemed to remember the dial growing big. She had thought she was falling through it …

"*Sophie!*" Chloe shouted. "Come on!

We'll miss the rest of the race!"

So Sophie stuffed the compass back into her pocket and hurried after her friend. She must have hit her head or something, she supposed. Bear and the desert had obviously all been her imagination.

Everyone was waiting at the next obstacle for the runners to come along the track. There were two logs lying on the ground, one for each team, about ten feet long. The runners had to walk from one end to the other while the logs tried to roll underneath them. If they fell off, then they had to start again.

It was Omar's turn to take the baton from Fatima. He was hopping up and down with impatience.

Sophie joined the others shouting

encouragement to Fatima. She didn't make it across the log the first time, or the second. Or the third … but neither did the boy on the Red team. The volume of cheers and shouts went up a notch every time one of them fell off.

Sophie thought Omar might explode with frustration.

"Just run!" Omar bellowed. "You don't need to stay on it all the way, just get near enough to me!"

On Fatima's fourth try she did it. She took Omar's advice and ran along the log with the baton held out in front of her, so that Omar could take it before she stumbled off. Her other arm was waving frantically for balance.

But the Red boy had also followed Omar's advice, and his arm was a little longer. He handed their baton over half a second before Omar could grab the baton from Fatima. The two boys raced away down the track, with Omar a bit behind.

Everyone headed off through the woods to the next handover point. As they walked, Sophie pulled her scarf off and shook it to get rid of the trapped sand. She was still itching from it. Then she used the scarf to brush her neck down and remove any last pieces of grit. Then –

But there wasn't another "then." She was staring at the scarf, and realizing something shocking.

She hadn't been wearing a scarf when she fell off the zip line.

This was the shemagh that Bear had given her.

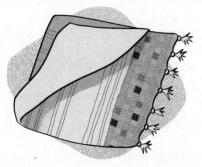

10

IN IT TO WIN IT

"Sophie! Come on!" Fatima called impatiently. "Chloe's on the last leg. Don't you want to cheer her?"

"Coming," Sophie called. She wanted to figure out the mystery of the scarf a lot more than she wanted to watch some race.

But she didn't want to let her friends down, so she hurried with Fatima to the handover point.

When he came around the corner, Omar had gained the lead – but only just. His face was bright red and his arms and legs were pumping.

Chloe for the Yellow team and Charlie for the Reds were waiting at the end of a pair of plastic pipes. The runners had to crawl through them. Omar dived headfirst into his pipe without stopping. A couple of seconds later, the baton was the first thing to emerge.

"Now, run! *Run!*" he screamed at Chloe. Chloe took the baton, turned, ran – and tripped right over a root hidden under the leaves.

She landed with a thump and a cry. The baton flew through the air, straight at Sophie. Sophie caught it automatically.

"*GET UP!*" Omar yelled. He couldn't

control his anger. He'd worked so hard to catch up and now they were going to lose. He looked as if he would explode. But Chloe's face was twisted with pain and she was holding her knee. It was obvious she wasn't going anywhere.

Charlie was already on his way, disappearing down the track. And Sophie had the baton. She took a step forward to help Chloe, but her friend waved her away.

"I'll be fine. You've got the baton! Use it!"

Sophie held it up for the umpire to see. "Can I …?

He nodded, and Sophie ran. She

was going to do this part of the race to her best ability – and she was going to do it for Chloe.

She fled down the track, pursued by the shouts of the Yellows.

Charlie was just disappearing around a bend. Her feet pounded after him. The trees shot past. The cheers were just a roar in her ears. Sophie came around the bend just in time to see Charlie's back disappear around the next one. She had gotten a little closer. She could do this!

She stepped up the pace until her feet were a blur beneath her.

One more bend, and there it was. The final clearing. Charlie hadn't realized how close behind Sophie was. He had slowed down and was just jogging to the finish, cheered on by his team. Their cheers suddenly turned to shouts of warning. Sophie was still going full pelt and she didn't slow down. Charlie shot her a look of alarm and started to speed up, but she had already overtaken him.

But there wasn't a finishing line. Just one of the leaders standing next to a table with two plastic tubs. IN IT TO WIN IT was painted on the side of each in large red letters.

There was something in the tub that Sophie needed to win the race. One last obstacle. She took a look inside her tub and paused just long enough for Charlie to catch up.

"Oh, gross!" he exclaimed.

It was full to the brim
with maggots. Live,
writhing maggots,
like zombie rice trying
to escape.

Charlie's hand hovered
over his tub for
just a second. A second
too long.

Sophie remembered
Bear's words.

"Don't knock a
maggot!" she said, and
plunged her hand straight in. The
maggots felt dry, and a bit tickly.

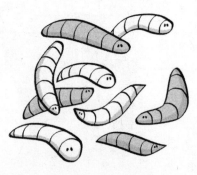

She felt the prize,
and pulled it out.
Behind her,
the Yellows

exploded into whoops and yells of victory.

It was just a laminated card that said WINNER, but Sophie was so pleased that it could have been made of solid gold. She hadn't let the team down – and bugs didn't scare her anymore!

"Yellow wins!" the umpire announced. Everyone gathered around Sophie, all giving hugs and high fives.

Almost everyone.

Omar came over to Sophie.

"Well done on winning," he grunted. "Only, we were twenty-two seconds off the record. We could have gotten that too, if you hadn't fallen off. There's a special prize for beating the record."

"Oh, well," Sophie said lightly. "We did our best, and we won the race."

Omar glared at her.

"Not the point," he muttered and stormed off.

The leaders then broke open a crate of snacks for everyone. People were chatting and laughing in the free time before the next activity, but Omar stayed away.

Eventually, Sophie took a juice carton over to him.

"Like a drink, Omar?" she asked.

"Thanks," he muttered. His bad temper seemed to have gone.

"You know ..." Sophie wasn't sure what to say, but she wanted to say *something*. "You took the race pretty seriously, didn't you?"

"I just …" he snapped, then stopped. Sophie was surprised to see tears in his eyes, before he quickly looked away. "I just like to win. Is that so bad? I just want to win – whatever the cost. So why am I *always* surrounded by slowpokes?!"

He stormed away.

Sophie watched him go. Those tears. It obviously *was* more than simply wanting to win. Something was really upsetting him.

She took the compass out of her pocket and looked thoughtfully at it.

Her adventure in the desert had been real. She knew it. She had the shemagh to prove it. The compass had taken her to a guy who could help her

get over the problem that was holding her back. And now she wasn't afraid of bugs anymore.

Maybe it could help someone else?

And if she was wrong, what was the worst that could happen? She might look bad. But not as bad as all the times she had screamed at an insect.

And so she followed after him.

"Hey, Omar?" she called softly.

She held the compass out to him.

"I just want to give you this," she said.

He looked at it, confused.

Sophie said with a smile, "Just consider it a gift …"

The End

Bear Grylls got the taste for adventure at a young age from his father, a former Royal Marine. After school, Bear joined the Reserve SAS, then went on to become one of the youngest people to ever climb Mount Everest, just two years after breaking his back in three places during a parachute jump.

Among other adventures he has led expeditions to the Arctic and the Antarctic, crossed oceans and set world records in skydiving and paragliding.

Bear is also a bestselling author and the host of television programs such as *Survival School* and *The Island*.

He has shared his survival skills with people all over the world, and has taken many famous movie stars and sports stars on adventures – and even President Barack Obama!

Bear Grylls is Chief Scout to the UK Scouting Association, encouraging young people to have great adventures, follow their dreams and to look after their friends.

When Bear's not traveling the world, he lives with his wife and three sons on a barge in London, or on an island off the coast of Wales.

Find out more at **www.beargrylls.com**

TEST YOUR DESERT SURVIVAL KNOWLEDGE!

1 When should you never try to walk in the desert?
a) in the morning
b) in the middle of the day
c) in the evening

2 What is a wadi?
a) a canteen
b) a beetle
c) a dry riverbed

3 How do you scare off snakes in the sand?
a) sing as you walk
b) walk with firm, steady steps
c) kick up the sand with each step

4 How can you find water in the desert?
a) wait for a rainstorm
b) look for an oasis with a lake and a palm tree
c) look for a plant and dig down under the earth

DID YOU KNOW?

Fog-basking beetles collect dew
to drink by sticking their bottoms
in the air on frosty desert mornings!

An ancient army of 50,000 soldiers
is believed to have been buried alive
during a sandstorm 2,500 years ago
in Egypt's Western Desert.

An adult desert tortoise can survive
for more than a year without water!

Antartica is the coldest place on Earth, but
it is also the largest desert in the world.
Only 20% of deserts are covered in sand.

ANSWERS

1: b) Never walk in the middle of the day when the sun is hottest.
2: c) A wadi is a dry riverbed.
3: b) Place your feet down firmly to make vibrations that warn snakes to move.
4: c) All plants need water, so dig half a foot or so under the surface to find their source.

Experience all the adventures ...

AVAILABLE NOW